T0319188

The Winners of Tomorrow

(a novella)

13 Years +

By

George Njimele

"On the whole, the characters, plot, subject matter and the themes are just fine. The themes are particularly relevant to the Cameroonian contemporary society." Dr Eleanor Dasi

"The characters have strong, distinct personalities; word choice is varied; there are strong themes throughout; the dialogue flows well…" Emily Kline.

"The plot and characters are thoroughly consistent throughout the story. The characterisation is concrete and builds an instant connection with the reader. The themes are crystal clear from the very beginning and are absolutely relevant to the story. The story is perfect as it clearly addresses the issues of today's world and delivers extremely needed morals to today's youth…" Tehniat Shuja.

Peacock Writers Series

P.O. Box 3092 Bonaberi, Douala, Cameroon

Tel: (+237) 677 52 72 36

Email: georgenjimele@gmail.com

First published 2023

© Peacock Writers Series

ISBN: 978 – 9956 – 540 – 21 - 1

Cover design: Rostand Blaise

Book formatting: Lawrence Ngwain.

Cover illustration: Franck Fokam

About the author

Njimele was born in Awing, North West Region Cameroon in 1973. He started writing at an early age, and he writes mostly for children and young adults. He took up writing full-time and started the Peacock Writers Series Cameroon. He won the National Prize for poetry in 1995 organized by the National Book Development Council. Some of his works such as *Madmen and Traitors* (2015), *The Queen of Power* (1998), *Undeserved Suffering* (2008), *The Slave Boys* (2008) and *Poverty is Crazy* (2012) are prescribed in the Cameroon school curriculum (literature awareness) for beginners in secondary school. His other works include: *King Shaba* (2006), *House of Peace* (2007), *Land of Sweet Meat* (2017), *A Time to Reconcile* (2020), *Nyamsi and His Grandson (2020)* and *Reap What You Sow* (2020).

Acknowledgements

Having a concept and turning it into a book is not an easy matter. Though the experience is challenging, it is rewarding as well. Without the support of line editors, developmental editors, proof-readers, illustrators, designers and typesetters, this book would not exist. Special thanks to Dr Eleanor Dasi, Emily Kline, Tarla Frankline, Eric Myers, Nganjo Nformi, Tehniat Shuja, Rostand Blaise, Franck Fokam and Lawrence Ngwain.
I thank my family, friends and all those who taught me.

Table of Contents

Chapter One

Mona and His Friend are Bullied

Mona knew the area surrounding his school was unsafe at certain times, yet he took the chance anyway. As he left the school late one evening with his friend, they took the meandering road down the slope. They trudged towards the south-eastern side of the school, chatting and feeling free. Midway to the riverbank, two bullies sauntered out of the bush and stopped in front of them. Mona and his friend froze when they recognised the boys. "We are dead!" Mona whispered.

Mona was scared of bullies. Slightly built and lacking in physical strength, he befriended muscular boys, believing they would rescue him in case he got attacked. Mona and his friend had stayed late in class to do their homework after school closed.

"That's Cobra," Pako said. Their faces turned ashen. Cobra and his friend stalked forward, pulling sharp knives from their belt loops. Cobra seized Mona by the collar and held a knife to his throat. Mona swallowed, unable to speak. Cobra turned his head and spat to the side.

"Surrender your phone! Quickly, or else I will squeeze your coconut head!" he roared.

"I have no phone," Mona said, blinking tears away. Cobra smelt of cannabis and fermented ginger drink. It was Mona's first time being attacked by Cobra, though he knew Cobra was a senior student who bullied everyone in the school. Cobra's friend seized five hundred francs from Pako.

"Boy, do not waste my time! I will peel off your skin if you don't comply," Cobra said. He searched Mona at knifepoint and grabbed a coin from one of his pockets.

"This guy is damn poor," he said, tossing the coin. Mona's heart raced. Cobra motioned to his friend to watch out. Someone was approaching. They saw someone descending from the hilltop. As the figure drew closer, it turned out to be a tall man with beefy arms. Frightened, the bullies turned on their heels and ran off. The burly man comforted the school children. "Make sure you report them to your principal," he advised. "They are lucky I didn't meet them." He dangled an arm as though aiming to hit a target, then he went off. Anger burned in Mona's and Pako's hearts. "The monsters have fled," Mona said.

"Sango took my money."
"How much?" Mona asked.
"Five hundred francs."
"Cobra took one hundred francs from my pocket."

"I heard him lamenting that you are poor."

"They are very wicked. Birds of a feather flock together," Pako said.

"We fell into their trap because we were alone."

That evening, Pako's father, Mr Pefok, came to see Ma Tata. He was fuming. Mr Pefok taught geography at Government High School Kibanki. He wondered where Cobra and his friend plucked up the courage to bully his son.

"I can't believe it!" he shouted. "Those boys are daredevils. They have no fear about the outcome of their actions."

"Don't bother yourself. I will see your principal tomorrow morning. What they have done is criminal, and we must seek justice for our children," Ma Tata assured.

"I can't wait for tomorrow! I am going to his house right away," Mr Pefok said, shaking his head.

"Acting fast is good, Mr Pefok. They may hurt someone next time."

Late that evening, when Pa Tata learnt that his son had been bullied, he gnashed his teeth in anger. "If they risk attacking teachers' children, they must have had a hidden agenda."

"They deserve dismissal. I will see their principal first thing in the morning."

Ma Tata impatiently tapped her foot. "They have twisted the lion's tail."

Chapter Two

Ma Tata Meets the Principal

Ma Tata ascended the slope leading to her son's school with soldierly speed the next morning. With a tight face and stern eyes, she walked on, hoping to meet the principal. A misty wind blew the tree branches and swept leaves along the ground. She wrapped her thick shawl round her neck to keep out the freezing cold. As birds chirped from the shrubs, roosters took turns letting out their last crows, announcing the break of a new day.

Mona trudged behind his mother at a brisk pace, though hardly fast enough to catch up with her. "Cobra and his friend have poked their fingers into fire," Ma Tata said, her nostrils flaring. "Ha! They have tried my anger, and a terrible reward awaits them." As she spoke, her breath fogged in the cold air. In her haste, she had left her pullover at home. The cold was fierce, but she endured it.

They got to the school and headed straight to the principal's office. His Mercedes 300 stood glittering in front of the building. "Thank God, he is already here," Ma Tata said, glancing at the car. She entered the principal's secretariat and met a gorgeously dressed secretary.

"Welcome, madam. What can I do for you?" the

secretary asked.

"I want to see the principal," Ma Tata responded.

"OK, wait for a minute. Please, have a seat. Ma Tata remained standing. The secretary entered Ma Tata's name in the visitor's book, then she rose, knocked on the principal's office door, and entered. When she came out, she said, "Please be patient. He'll be with you shortly."

"Good morning, Madam Tata," a male teacher greeted her.

"Good morning, my dear," she answered. She didn't know the teacher. She thought he must know her because of her leadership position in the Teachers' Trade Union.

Another teacher, a senior staff member, noticed her presence, came over, and shook hands with her. "It's a pleasure to meet you, ma'am," she said, smiling. "You will be rewarded for what you're doing to improve our working conditions." Ma Tata smiled at her and they hugged each other. The teacher patted Mona on the back. "Your son is curious and stays focused. He's polite and well-behaved." Ma Tata's eyes crinkled at the woman's kind words about her son. Other teachers greeted her, and she returned their greetings with warmth, though she knew none of them.

Mona stood quietly staring at his mum, feeling pleased with her fame and the honour bestowed on her by his teachers. His mother wielded more influence than his father. Ma Tata was pushy, brave, and stern.

She had a strong sense of justice. She stood by her word and was ready to die for it. On the other hand, Pa Tata was cool and calm, but meticulous in conducting his affairs.

The secretary ushered Ma Tata into the principal's office. Upon seeing her, the principal, Mr Komso, rose and shook her hand, smiling affectionately, showing his grey front teeth. They had met in several pedagogic meetings before and took a moment to exchange pleasantries. Mona recognised his mother's distinguished status. Mr Komso hardly received parents in his office, except in special cases. He delegated his vice or the senior master of discipline to attend to most parents. Rising and shaking hands with Ma Tata spoke volumes. Mona proudly held his chin high.

"Mr Komso, I have come to make a complaint against two of your students," Ma Tata said, fixing her shawl as she got to the point of her visit.

"Oh? What is the matter, Ma Tata?" Mr Komso asked. Ma Tata cleared her throat and stood straight. "My son and his friend were bullied yesterday by two of your students, who took their money." The principal's eyes widened in surprise. Ma Tata thought Mr Pefok had briefed him on the bullying incident.

"My goodness! Two students from this school, you mean?"

"Yes, sir." Mr Komso shifted his chair forward, turned to Mona, and asked,

"Do you know the students who bullied you and took your money?"

"Yes, sir."

"Who were they?"

"Cobra and Sango."

"Cobra! Truly, there's something in a name. Your name tells who you are. Cobra must be a venomous snake, I suppose."

"Sure, sir. There's a similar practice in my school. Headstrong students take evil names and end up being evil," Ma Tata said.

Mr Komso flashed his hawkish eyes at the ceiling.

"Tell us in detail what they did to you," he continued.

"I left the school in the afternoon and was on my way back home with my friend Pako. Somewhere down the slope, Cobra and Sango came out of the bush, held knives to us and took our money." Mr Komso clenched his teeth and struck the table with his fist.

"That's horrible! These children are turning into something else."

"We are facing similar problems in my own school," Ma Tata said.

"If you see Cobra and Sango, can you point them out?" the principal asked.

"Yes, sir. Cobra is in lower sixth, and Sango is in upper sixth," Mona said.

"Senior students!" he exclaimed. "How much money did they take from you?"

"Cobra took one hundred francs from me, and Sango took five hundred francs from Pako."

"The amount does not matter; a crime is a crime. It's OK, get to class. I will call you later." Mona left the office and headed to class, thinking about the likely outcome of the bullying incident. Corporal punishment had been forbidden in schools. Would they be subjected to hard labour instead? Would they be dismissed outright? Mona feared for his life and that of his friend. Punishing the bullies might be more trouble than it was worth. He feared the boys might take revenge if they were punished because of him and Pako.

Mr komso diverted the topic, perhaps to ease Ma Tata's anxiety.

"Ma Tata, your son speaks English well."

"He is the son of a teacher," Ma Tata said, half smiling.

"I know children of teachers who barely speak well."

"I make a lot of effort to teach him English."

"I hope you also teach him the local language as well."

"Yes of course. He speaks my language."

Mr Komso nodded. "We must promote our own local languages," he said.

Ma Tata looked towards the window and then

glanced at her watch.

"Sir, I think these students deserve dismissal."

"I dismiss students here every week. Last week, I dismissed three students who were caught acting in a pornographic film in an uncompleted building. The week before last, I dismissed two others for attempting to knife their mates in school. I am investigating a case of a female student assaulting a teacher. If found guilty, she will be dismissed. I'll investigate Cobra and Sango. If they deserve dismissal, I won't hold back the decision of the disciplinary council."

"It's the same scenario everywhere, sir. In my school, students are involved in substance abuse, sex scandals and violence. It's a trend. Modern technologies have brought us many problems. Our children have become scammers, law abusers, drug lords and addicts, sex predators, porn stars, and pitiless monsters."

"Madam, I thought dismissals would deter crime, but it is not the case. Those dismissed get more involved in their crimes. Dismissal to some is a mere gateway to more lawlessness."

"I have to go, sir. Before I leave, I must stress that dismissal is the only solution in this matter. We will discuss more some other time. I have something urgent to do."

"All right. As promised, I will investigate Cobra and Sango and get back to you." The principal rose and walked Ma Tata out.

Chapter Three

The Bullies are Dismissed

Students flocked into the yard Friday morning from various parts of the town, beads of sweat dripping down their faces from the long trek. Every morning, the school gate was flung open from six to eight. Those arriving at past eight were punished as late coming was not tolerated. Most students made efforts to be punctual, yet they kept coming late. Many of them lived far away, and only a few used taxis or motorbikes to get to school. Transport fares had gone up because of unstable fuel prices.

Mona loved his school because of its mission statement. The school's management created it to instil a new way of life, and assure growth and change in its students. They said the school to every learner was like a fountain of water to young plants. Mona was happy to be part of those who poured in daily, longing to know more about themselves, nature, life, and the world at large. They herded into the yard to transform their minds from lower levels of reasoning to advanced thinking.

Other students did not appreciate the school the way Mona did. Some snuck out of their classes, jumped over the fence, and loitered in the quarters. To stop the practice, the yard was fenced off with a concrete wall, tall enough to deter anyone from scaling it.

When the bell rang for assembly time, Mona joined other students congregating on the assembly ground. They stood in rows according to their classes. The school prefects paced the corridors, instructing everyone to make haste. The principal emerged from the staff entrance, holding a manila folder in his hand. With lion-like grace, he walked to the assembly ground and stood beside the platform.

The first speaker was the male senior prefect, who posed as though ready for a snapshot. Dressed in a properly ironed uniform, he flashed his golden-brown eyes as he spoke. He said a short prayer, made some announcements, and then conducted the singing of the national anthem. The senior master of discipline took over and reminded students, as usual, to be punctual and disciplined. The principal mounted the platform as the last speaker. Everyone was attentive. His presence always brought awe and suspicion. His face was rigid, his eyes enraged.

Mr Komso had barely been the principal for two years. He inherited the school when it was in bad shape. There old buildings were collapsing, and their cracked walls bore faded paints. Brown zinc sheets covered the roofs, and rusted nails and rotten planks hung above the ceilings. Though cemented, the floors had porous layers brought about by the burdens of walking feet. The lawns were barren, lacking greenery and flowers.

Mr Komso met a school with unchecked students. Girls freely wore bushy braids, painted lips, high-heeled shoes and tight-fitting skirts. The boys grew long beards, displayed scary hairstyles, and wore baggy or close-fitting uniforms according to individual tastes.

As the new principal, Mr Komso had been told that his predecessor, Dr Mbang, was the cause of all the school's problems. Dr Mbang had studied in Britain and obtained a PhD in Botany. After his appointment as principal, he began showing off, telling people that everything British was flawless. He adored his old-fashioned short coat, which he wore every day. It was split in the back. Students believed it had been split with a blunt machete. Dr Mbang claimed it reminded him of his days in the University of Warwick in the UK. He tried speaking slightly accented English, but he blended English sounds with those of his mother tongue. He touted, "My monthly salary is half a million," and, "Call me Dr Mbang, not Mr Mbang."

Modestly dressed in his smart three-piece suit, the new principal looked younger than his age. His face was smooth and void of any birthmarks. He peered into his file and asked, "Where are Cobra and Sango?" The students laughed with surprise. The principal had never addressed students by their nicknames before. The female senior prefect checked various rows and told him, "They are absent, sir."

The principal nodded, opened a page in his documents and read out the school rules and regulations. He always did so each time he was announcing the verdict of the disciplinary council. He stated the rules broken by Cobra and Sango during the bullying incident. "I hereby dismiss them in absentia for unruly behaviour," he declared.

The assembly was drowned in an uproar. Form one students shrieked and jumped in happiness. Mona and Pako had mixed feelings.

Chapter Four

Mona's Fear is Gone

Mona remained timid and fearful the whole day after the dismissal. He did not even go to lunch. He remained in class during break time and ate the croquettes his mum had given him at home. When school ended for the day, he told Pako, "Let's get a taxi home."

"I don't have money," Pako complained. Pako was short, bulky, and had kinky hair and bandy legs. He was an easy-going fourteen-year-old.

"I will lend you money. You can pay me back. Let's not take chances. Cobra and Sango are wicked boys. They might hide in the bush and attack us."

"You're right," Pako said. "But for how long shall we live with this fear?"

"I will talk to my parents about the issue. They must seek a solution to it," Mona said. They boarded a taxi in front of the school and returned safely. Their mates knew their lives were at stake because they caused the dismissal of notorious bullies.

When Ma Tata came back from work, Mona welcomed her with the news. "Mum, Cobra and Sango were expelled from school today."

"They deserved it," Ma Tata said with a nod.

"Your principal called to inform me after

dismissing them. Before I left the office, I knew they would be dismissed. What they did to you was horrible." Mona dropped his head and pondered.

"Aren't you happy about their expulsion?" she asked.

"I am, but I am afraid they may attack us for revenge. We came back from school by taxi."

"That won't happen, for God's sake. I called Commissioner Teko and told him the whole story. He called Cobra's father and sternly warned him. He told him that Cobra will be jailed if he dares to touch you." Mona smiled and patted his mother's arm. "Carry on with your studies without fear. Take note, I told you I was not OK with your last results."

"Mum, I promise to do better next term. I came fifth with an average of fourteen, and I thought that was a brilliant performance."

"It was by your standards, of course! But the fifth position is not the first position. Those who come first don't carry horns on their heads. You are the son of a teacher. With all the privileges at your disposal, you are supposed to lead your class. During my student days, I never missed the first position. Your father always topped his class as well. You carry our genes of intelligence."

"By God, I will improve my result next term. The issue is that I don't like to memorise like the girl who always comes first. She crams while preparing for exams."

"I never did that during my studies," Ma Tata said.

"It is the worst method of studying. When you are employed, you apply what you studied at school. Those who memorise forget everything after exams and are never effective at work in the future."

"I also noticed that those occupying the first three positions are good at maths, English and French, which are high coefficient subjects."

"Everyone can be good at any subject. It is all about studying hard," Ma Tata advised.

Chapter Five

The Town of Kibanki

Mona heard loud pig grunts in the sty. He got a basket of ripe avocados and made for the sty. The female pig raised her snout and wagged her tail when she saw him. Mona winked at her, and she lifted her head.

"I know your problem. You've not eaten anything since morning." The fat sow had a flat mouth, a short tail, and cloven hooves. She had just turned ten a few days ago.

Six piglets snorted within the pigpen and ran to meet the sow. They stood by her, squealing and watching Mona as if pleading, "We are hungry; we want to eat." Mona climbed over the fence and threw the avocados to the pigs. They fell on the tasty food.

"You're wonderful creatures. You don't bother about laying the table during meals. You don't mind whether your food is peppered or not. I guess your tongues know nothing about the taste of *maggi*, salt, or ginger." When they finished devouring their dinner, the sow went and couched in her nest. The piglets followed her and gathered at her belly to suckle. They were just a few months old and could barely take care of themselves.

Mona observed the little pigs and exclaimed, "Ha, they

have just finished eating! Six piglets on her alone! No pity for their poor mum, eh!" He reached for a bucket, drew water from the well, and gave it to the pigs. Then he went off; they were catered for that day.

Milking cows by hand was a skill Mona wished to learn someday. To him, cow milk was pure, safe, and nourishing. One day, herders would teach him how to milk pacific cows. Mona had seen how it was done a couple of times, but he needed to practise it himself.

Mona loved pets and farm animals. Cats purring and rubbing themselves against his legs made him happy. He could imitate the calls of bulls, goats, camels, and sheep. He also knew sounds made by some domestic and wild birds. Doves' coos and crows' caws fascinated him. He loved seeing cows grazing in the fields or lying in the shades, resting and keeping cold. The African breeds of bulls attracted him with their soft and meaty hunchbacks. Mona liked hunchback beef because it was juicy and boneless. When it was added to *fufu* and yam, he could eat beyond his fill.

When Mona wasn't caring for the animals, he spent his spare time playing with his friends on the lands around their house. The place was a treasure to him.

Though not natives of Kibanki, the Tatas felt at home here. They had settled in Kibanki eight years ago, after Ma Tata transferred to teach in Government

Secondary School Kiti on the outskirts of Kibanki. Back then, Kibanki was a slum, with ramshackle houses, bumpy roads, withering vegetation, and contaminated water. Bare-chested and destitute children wandered along the streets, searching the smelly rubbish heaps for food. Cars queued up along the untarred roads, their tyres sticking in the red mud. In heavy traffic, impatient drivers shouted at those in front of them, honking in fury.

Over time, Kibanki transformed into a modern town with refurbished houses, trading centres, attractive hotels, schools, and churches. The Tatas had chosen a house at its border when they had moved. A lush yard with unpruned hedges surrounded the five-roomed house. Its owner was a military retiree living in another part of the town. Immense arable land extended down to a ravine to the house's right. Beside the ravine, a spring gushed out pure, fresh potable water. Herbalists visited the spring every weekend to purify sick and bewitched persons. When water was not running at the house's tap, Mona fetched it from the spring. Trees flanked the left side of the house. Bird nests hung in the foliage and branches. Though many of the trees blossomed, others looked withered from the harsh climate. Many leaves and tree branches were eaten up by webworms and black ants.

Chapter Six

Beware of the Thief!

Mona left school and headed home, his stomach rumbling with hunger. He kicked off his shoes without unlacing them when he got home, changed out of his uniform and hurried into the kitchen. His stomach rumbled again as he pulled open the fridge. "What has Mum cooked today?" His favourite dish sat beside a red casserole.

"Oh, this is great!" Mum had cooked aubergine soup and pounded yams. Mona liked broth soups, especially those made with stockfish, beef, and delicious spices.

Mona dished up a healthy serving of the soup and yams and sat on a wooden stool to eat. "Mum's the best cook," he said, salivating as he gazed at the soup and the appetising slices of beef in it. Mona balled up lumps of pounded yam, steeped them in the soup and devoured them. After eating, he drank two glasses of water to quench his thirst.

After cleaning up his dishes, he went outside to refresh himself in the cold evening air. His father had tended to the sow and the piglets. With no task at hand, Mona sat in the yard, gazing at bits of pumpkin and cucumber his father had scattered about for the chickens.

He watched the chicks pecking at leftover millet and beans. The roosters dropped their wings and danced to attract the hens, lizards basked on stones, and birds hovered overhead. "Animals are happy creatures," he remarked.

Looking towards the pigsty, he noticed a faint shadow wandering about. As Mona craned his neck to get a better view of the shadow, it transformed into his neighbour. "Oh, what's Pa Mo doing here?" Mona tiptoed forward. Upon seeing him, Pa Mo turned round and took off. Alarmed by his behaviour, Mona ran to the pigsty. Had any pigs been stolen?

All the pigs were safe. He followed Pa Mo's footprints. Pa Mo fled and vanished into the bush. Mona came back to the pigsty and recounted the pigs; they were all there. The piglets relaxed beside the sow. "What about the chickens?" Realising that Pa Mo had not stolen any of the chickens, he released a heavy breath.

Pa Tata approached the pigsty, carrying fresh weeds and cassava tubers in a basket. Dressed in a threadbare jumper over knee-level trousers, he resembled a herdsman. Mona got the feed and stored in the shed.

"Something terrible almost happened," Mona told his father.

"What was it?"

"Pa Mo was here."

"Doing what, my son?"

"I saw him loitering around the pigsty, but I didn't meet him face to face."

"Oh my God! I don't like when he comes here in my absence. He certainly thought no one was at home, and then came to steal our pigs."

"If I hadn't been there, he could have stolen all the pigs and the fowls."

"God forbid! Pa Mo will never stop stealing. He has been stealing for more than thirty years."

"Ha! Thirty years!"

"Yeah, if he were in a good profession, he could have got a labour medal."

"Dad, why is he not in prison?"

"Pa Mo is a smart thief. Each time he is charged with theft, he buys his way out."

"He is too old to still be stealing."

"Life is all about making choices. That's his choice."

"A bad choice, indeed! He looks miserable. It must all be the risk."

"Well, that's his problem. Please keep watching out. He has stolen a lot of farm animals from me in the past. Before you were born, I had donkeys, sheep, and goats. I also tended pets. He is a dog and cat eater, and that's why I don't tend dogs anymore and why we don't have pets. He has stolen from everyone here. We just have to be careful with him. He spends all his days thinking about how to grab what belongs to others."

Chapter Eleven

The Traders of Kibanki Market

With a handcrafted basket in hand, Ma Tata sped up to keep pace with the earliest buyers as she headed towards the market. Going late to the market meant choosing to buy junky foodstuffs. Dressed in a casual house gown, her dazzling eyes squinted and her hips wiggled as she walked. She preferred walking because the market was not far away from her house. Mona followed behind her with a knapsack strapped to his shoulder, panting and wiping away sweat on his face with a piece of cloth. They walked past shops and makeshift kiosks, greeting familiar persons with nods and hand waves. At the market centre, retailers cleaned the corridors and shelves.

A vendor paced back and forth, touting his wares in a melodious voice. "Buy your shoes here. I have a limited stock. I sell American and Italian shoes at cheap prices. Buy for yourself, for your son, or for your   girlfriend…"

Another vendor stood with a large bag on his shoulder, howling, "I sell French perfume and toiletries. Get your American toothpaste and shower gels at giveaway prices."

Ma Tata turned to his son and said, "Observe them very well. They are trying their best to earn a leaving." Mona watched the boys, thinking of what he would do if, by fate, he became a hawker.

"Mum, some of them live good lives and take good care of their families," Mona said.

"Yes, they make a lot of money from this business. Some of them own large houses. All jobs are important. Call for the boy selling toiletries," Ma Tata said. Mona motioned to the boy, who came running, afraid that a fellow trader could outmatch and outsell him.

"Let me see the toothpaste you sell," Ma Tata said, picking up one tube.

"Yes, madam, you have chosen the best. That's toothpaste from France. When you brush your teeth with it, it brightens them, and makes you look younger. It removes mouth odours, and you can use it for one full year…"

"What! One full year? Please, stop the comedy!" Ma Tata said. "You are a liar! You said it is made in France. Look at this. It is clearly written here, "Made in China." The salesboy lowered his chin in shame.

"It is a mistake, ma'am. I thought I still had the one from France. No problem." He reached into his bag and got out another type of toothpaste. "Madam, this one is superb. It befits someone of your calibre. It is from America!"

Chapter Seven

The Famous Teacher

Ma Tata dropped her handbag and slumped into the nearest lounge when she returned from work. "Water, please. My throat is so dry." Mona brought her a glass of water. She gulped down two glassfuls. After a bit of rest, she untied her booties and put on indoor slippers. Slowly, she took off her necklace, her bracelet, and earrings and dropped them into her jewellery box. Ma Tata wore red-brown lipstick, which smoothened her lips. She applied modest makeup ensuring it didn't attract much notice. Her ebony skin and grey hair shone with good health.

After a short while, she regained her energy, rose, and walked to find Mona.

"Mum, Pa Mo came to steal our pigs today," Mona told her.

"Oh my God! Pa Mo in our yard again? That old man should be ashamed of himself." She raised her hands in wonder.

"Thank God I was at home, keeping watch. I had come back from school, ate my lunch, and then saw him sneaking around the pigsty."

"Thanks be to God you saw him in time. But you are a student; you can't be on guard all the time. Pa Mo will come for the pigs when he notices you are at school. He knows when we are not at home. He knows when your father goes to buy the feed. He knows the work schedule of everyone in this neighbourhood."

"Mum, what can we do to safeguard the pigs?" Mona asked.

"I advised your father to recruit a full-time security guard. I think that's the best thing to do. Hiring a guard will cost us money, but it is worth it. Though your dad says the pigs and fowls bring little profit then. Well, when Pa Mo steals everything, I won't feel sorry."

Ma Tata took out a stack of test papers from her bag and laid them on the table. She got a red ballpoint pen, picked up the first paper, and checked through the answers.

"Mum, you haven't eaten anything. You can't continue working on an empty stomach."

"I ate at my colleague's house. She invited me to her birthday party. I am OK."

Marking test papers was not her favourite part of teaching. Delivering lessons was much easier than marking stacks of papers. An answer sheet with clumsy handwriting and off-topic answers was difficult to grade. It pleased her when a student answered a question in neat handwriting.

Each teaching session ended with an evaluation.

No teacher, however experienced, could skip the

evaluation stage. Though schools were invaded by teachers with less convictions, Ma Tata believed teaching would always remain the noblest profession. She would choose to be a teacher all over again if she could. "This student writes trash," she grumbled as she read through an answer sheet. "History is not all about narrating past events. I can't see facts in this essay." She gave the student a low score. Impertinent answers and poor presentation of facts eased her marking.

In her mid-forties, Ma Tata had taught history in secondary school for two decades. Because of her boldness and her love for fair play, her colleagues named her "Lioness." She had been the spokesperson for the National Teachers' Trade Union for ten years. The union advocated better pay for teachers, improved working conditions, good retirement benefits, and security in the workplace. Though her advocacy brought a few changes, she felt much was still to be done. Insecurity plagued schools across the country. Students robbed and attacked other students and even teachers. They fought with their mates and stole from the locals. Truants filmed pornography. They smoked cannabis, took tramadol and rampaged through the town. Ma Tata held face-to-to meetings with the minister of education to address the insecurity in schools. Many measures still awaited decisions.

Chapter Eight

The Food Shed

It was a bright morning in GHS Kibanki. The Sun's rays flashed and brightened the lush greenery of the schoolyard. The school playfield bustled with activity. Fresh from primary school, form one students had more energy for violent and risky play. They jumped over flowerbeds, leapt over tables and benches, twisted their mates' ears, and pulled and pushed each other. They played without precaution and soiled their uniforms and shoes. The school prefects tired of calling them to order. The senior students simply watched them with contempt, trying to relive their own memories. They, too, had been into such childlike play at that age. Sometimes, form one students obeyed instructions in a brief moment, then returned to their wrongdoings the next.

Many students had come out for long break. Others stayed in to copy notes or do their homework. Some remained in class because they could not afford money for lunch. Some simply opted to remain in class and gossip about other students and teachers. Almost every teacher had been given a well-crafted nickname by the students.

Mr Konte, the first cycle chemistry teacher, was called "Duodenum." His colleague, Monsieur Kouam of the French department, was nicknamed "Cher Camarade." Students hated strict teachers. On the contrary, gentle, kind and easy-going teachers were loved. All masters of discipline were looked upon as serpents with venomous fangs.

The food shed was full of students wrestling to eat lunch. "Serve me first," one student said.

"I came before you," another one retorted. The sellers endured the students' arguments to make their day's wages. Some of the students were cunning and deceitful. They took advantage of the overcrowding by eating their food and leaving without paying for it. The principal received several complaints about cheating and stealing by students and meted out sanctions accordingly.

The food sellers were authorised to sell beans, buns, and rice. According to the principal, nothing else could be sold apart from these, and all food sellers must identify themselves by wearing aprons. They had to provide to the school a medical certificate (no more than six months old) signed by a competent medical doctor in service with the Ministry of Public Health. The master of discipline inspected the food sheds every morning to make sure they were kept tidy.

As punishment, late comers cleaned up the sheds.

Mona got to the food shed at break time and ordered rice and beans. He didn't mind the limited menu like some other students did. Though black beans sometimes made his belly rumble, it only happened in rare instances.

"Don't add pepper," he told Mami Chop as she spooned his rice and beans onto a plate.

Mona had come early enough to secure a tiny space at the edge of the lone bench in the shed. Because of limited seating, some students squatted. Others leaned against the stilts supporting the shed. Mami Chop feared the stilts may one day break, collapsing the shed. Mona got his food and ate like a soldier at war. He chewed the grains thrice and swallowed, though taking care not to choke himself. They served brown beans today, his favourite type of beans. As for rice, he knew nothing about the different varieties on the market. Whether it was from China, Thailand or India, all rice was the same to him.

Midway into eating, he turned to the seller and said, "Mami Chop, you promised me a spoonful of rice and beans last week." Mami Chop lifted her head and gazed at him.

"Ah, I remember. But, Can't you forget? Beans are very expensive, my son. But I must honour my promise." She ladled a good quantity of rice and beans and added them to Mona's plate. All eyes turned on Mona.

"Ha, Mami Chop, stop discriminating!" said one student.

"I am not favouring anyone, my son.
I promised him," Mami replied.
"Promise me too," said the student.
"Hahaha! No problem, remind me on   Friday."
"Mami Chop, promise me too," said another student.

"No, please! Beans are expensive. The price of beans is going up every day," she explained. The student's face became tight.

"Expensive, eh? When it comes to me, everything becomes expensive! No problem." Mami Chop ignored him and collected her money from some students. Since many students were in the habit of eating food and walking away without paying, Mami Chop had created rules to prevent the losses she incurred from such students. Several notices hung on the stilts on which was inscribed "Payment before service" This was a sure way to avoid bad debts.

The school bell rang with a deafening sound, announcing that break time was over. The old metallic bell had been replaced with an electric one.

The new bell echoed several miles away. It was a veritable tool of intimidation. No student defied its authority. In the twinkle of an eye, the food sheds emptied.

The form one students stopped playing and scurried into their various classes. The senior master of discipline stood at the centre of the schoolyard with his feet spread apart. He was a disciplinary expert with decades on the job and four labour medals to his name.

He flashed his eyes about to intimidate sluggish students. In his right hand was a whip, which he waved to and fro. No student dared to challenge his authority.

Chapter Nine

The Suspicious Visitor

Ma Tata had prepared a study timetable for Mona. It paid particular attention to core subjects with high coefficients.

"You must respect the schedule by studying every day, " she insisted.

When Mona came back from school, he ate his dinner and sat relaxing for a moment. He glimpsed at the bronze wall clock and exclaimed, "Oh, it is study time already!" According to the timetable, he was supposed to study maths. He knew Ma Tata would realise it if he failed to study. He hurried to the living room, opened his maths book, and was reading through it.

The modestly furnished room contained mahogany chairs, an enormous dining table, and woven Chinese carpets. The last bit of the day's sun shone in through the casement windows. Distracted by the noise, Mona turned off the TV standing in the corner and studied in earnest. He switched off his mobile phone as well and laid it on the table. Mum had barred him from watching TV during study hours. She also forbade him from watching anything she felt could taint his morals.

Pa Tata returned home and noticed that water

was running at the tap and flooding the veranda.

"What's this?" he roared.

Mona rushed out and turned off the tap. "The tap water was not running this morning. I turned it on to check and forgot to turn it off."

"So much water has been wasted," Pa Tata said, gnashing his teeth. Mona stood silent, remorseful.

"For five consecutive months, we have suffered from water shortages in this town. Every day, the Water Utility Corporation blames shortages on low water volume at the dams. They say because of limited rainfall, water volumes at the cascades are low. How that is our business, I don't know. Aren't we paying our bills?" The chickens ran after him, cackling.
"Have these birds eaten?"

"Yes, I gave them maize."

Pa Tata got more maize and threw it in the yard. The chickens swooped on the food, fighting as each struggled to get a good share.

Mona got tied down to work, revising his history lessons. He focused on history because Ma Tata taught history, and he feared she might ask him questions he didn't know the answers. Pa Tata tossed his wallet into the room, made for the kitchen, and reached into the fridge for a gourd of palm wine. It was slightly fermented wine, thick, and yellow. He poured some into a black honed cup and sat on a stool in the centre of the yard. Pa Tata gazed at the drink before him. He tasted the wine, gulped it, and refilled the cup. The sun had fallen and the birds shrieked and headed to their roosts. Pa Tata sat alone, serenely enjoying his drink.

"Good evening, Pa Tata," Pa Mo said as he approached him. Pa Tata startled and turned his head towards the voice.

"Welcome," he greeted. Pa Mo settled on the ground, yawned, and stretched. Pa Tata got a bamboo cup for his visitor and poured some wine into it. Pa Mo was an old man with age spots and a furrowed face. His eyes were red like those of drunkards, and his teeth broken, maybe from eating too many kola nuts.

Pa Mo tasted the wine. Brightening, he sat upright. "This is good wine." He emptied his cup in a quick gulp, then stretched it out for more.

"Where do you get this?"

"It's straight from the village. I have a boy who supplies it to me every week."

"Please, connect me with the boy."

"I promise to connect you with him."

"Don't break the promise, please. I like the wine because it is not too sweet."

"That's because it's pure. Everything else is adulterated: drugs, kerosene, gasoil, red oil, vegetable oil, detergents, and so on. I don't know where we are heading to," Pa Tata said. Mona tiptoed and stood at the door, peeping and listening to them. He cast an evil eye at Pa Mo, frowned and returned to his work.

"Pa Tata, I learnt some daring students attacked and took money from your son and his friend. It that true?" Pa Mo asked.

"It's true. That happened a few days ago."

"I am lost for words, Pa Tata. Our children are becoming impatient and unruly."

"Our society is rotten from top to bottom. And who do we blame? The founders of the land, without doubt. And who are the founders of the land? The leaders! If we choose to eat spoilt kola nuts rather than fine ones, our children will imitate us. We are mixing lies with the truth, and that is where we've gone totally wrong."

"What was done to the wayward bullies?"

"What else do you expect? They were dismissed. But let's be frank, Pa Mo, was that a pertinent solution? It didn't solve the bigger problem. They will join the gangs and make our lives more miserable. They will dream of moving to Europe, then take to the deserts engaging in lawless sex and making bastards, sharing in the food of apes, dying in the torturous hands of Arab infidels and extremist militias. Dozens will die in the Mediterranean Sea, and their bodies will never be recovered for decent burials. Pa Mo, that's where we find ourselves."

"So sad indeed!" Pa Mo said. "We are living fearful days. It never was like this. In the beginning, our forebears lived modest lives in peace and goodness. Each person was their neighbour's keeper. We had no tricky politics or dangerous calculations. This new way of life has robbed our children of their moral values. Where does a student get money to buy a flashy car for himself? Where do they get money to live exuberant lives?"

"Pa Mo, suffice it to say you didn't grasp what I said earlier. Let me repeat. If the guardians are bad, the kids in their care will be the same. If the care-givers in a foster home are evil-minded people, those under their tutelage won't be different. Why are our kids bearing risks in the seas and in the deserts? They want to improve themselves. Why are they fleeing their fatherland? It's because we failed to plan for them. It's because no one cares. They have been abandoned to themselves. We are not models to them, to say the least. The shame is on us all."

Pa Mo held a finger to his jaw and pondered. He emptied his cup and said, "I am going back." Pa Tata wished him well but did not bother to see him out. Mona noticed the visitor leaving and came out. He watched Pa Mo to make sure he wasn't going to the pigsty to steal. Mona walked down to the pigsty and stood guard for some minutes before getting back to his studies.

Chapter Ten

Who Owns the Best Car?

Mona hated getting punished for tardiness. He feared oversleeping and losing track of time, so he set the alarm clock for five in the morning. His eyes snapped open when it blared, and he tossed the blanket aside. After turning off the alarm, he pulled the edge of the window blind and looked outside. Darkness shrouded the yard and the trees nearby. A faint light shone from the security bulb at the corridor. He tried getting up, but his body resisted as if exhausted from a nightmarish battle with beasts before the crack of dawn.

A rooster crowed in the backyard, telling him it was time to get out of bed. He must, or he would be late for school. At last, he rose from bed, scratching his head and rubbing his eyes.

Ma Tata was in the kitchen, dishes clinking as she prepared breakfast. She had got up earlier than everyone else. Pa Tata had gone to get feed for the pigs and the chickens. "Where are you, Mona?" Ma Tata asked.

"I am in the room, Mum, arranging my books."

"Do that fast, or you will be late to school."

Mona had two chores in the morning: mopping the sitting room floor and feeding the pigs.

Mona finished both tasks within an hour. He showered with cold water, then dressed up in khaki trousers and a sky-blue shirt. He put on white socks and black sandals before heading to the kitchen for breakfast: fried plantains with tea.

"Put some of the plantain chips in your bag for lunch," Ma Tata instructed.

Mona looked at the time and ate quickly, then left for school. It was foggy outside, and the rain threatened to fall. He was not sure of what he would do if it started raining. He did not trust the weather forecast broadcasted on TV every morning. Some days the forecaster said the weather would be bright, but by mid-day, rain poured down in torrents.

Mona hurried to school through the fog. Most teachers were already in school. As he walked through the parking lot, he admired the sparkling cars in front of the principal's office.

Mona loved cars and wanted to buy the flashiest type when he finished school and got a job. All the cars at the school were family cars with low horsepower. The most conspicuous among them was the glistening, Swedish-designed Volvo owned by Mr Atanga, a first-cycle biology teacher. It was a fancy five-seater with an automatic transmission, air-conditioning, airbags, and a multi-function steering wheel.

Mona adored the car's owner as much as the car. Mr Atanga was a flamboyant teacher with an MSc in biology obtained from Fourah Bay University, Sierra Leone. He liked expensive Italian shoes, leather jackets, and trousers. He also fancied bright-coloured woollen shirts ordered from foreign designers. Claiming to be of noble birth, he expected everyone to honour and glorify him accordingly. His car set him apart from others, giving him aristocratic airs. Other teachers made modest choices of less-expensive Japanese Toyota cars.

Mona got to class and sat in his usual position: the front centre of the classroom. The bell rang for the first lesson. The geography teacher, Miss Penda, was not yet around. The class buzzed with excitement. The senior master of discipline heard the noise, came to the window, and ordered, "Give me the names of all the noisemakers!" The class prefect stood and rattled the names of eight students who had been speaking. "Follow me!" the master of discipline roared. When they reached him, he pulled and twisted the ears of two of them, and they yelled in pain.

Mona, too, had been making noise, but he had not been caught. Feeling lucky, he smiled and picked up his French exercise book to study.

Miss Penda came to class ten minutes late. The class prefect bashed the desk, and all the students rose in greeting. "Sit!" she said. Mona did not rise on time and Miss Penda noticed it. "You, stand up!" she ordered. Mona got up, gripping his book with shaking hands. "Come and kneel here!" Mona obeyed her and knelt in the front of the class.

Miss Penda introduced her lesson and began teaching. After a few minutes, the noisemakers returned. Miss Penda glared at them, ordered them to sit, and then resumed her lesson. Mona fidgeted. He laid his hands on the bare floor to relieve his pain. His knees, too, were hurting. Some of his mates giggled at him, and Miss Penda noticed that he was distracting the class. She turned to him and said, "Get up! Next time I will ask you to run round the school a hundred times." Mona went back to his seat.

He scowled at those who giggled at him, then took his pen in hand and tried to catch up with the lesson. "Please, may I see your notes?" he pleaded with his neighbour.

"I am not done yet," the neighbour said, shaking his head. Mona turned to another mate on his left. "Please, may I see your notes?" he begged.

The student pitied him. "Copy them for two minutes, then give back my book." Mona grabbed the book and smiled at him.

A while later, the bell sounded, announcing the end of the lesson. Miss Penda signed the logbook and made for the door. She exchanged greetings with the French teacher, who stood there waiting to enter.

At short break, he sat at his desk drawing biology diagrams and solving maths problems. During long break, he still remained in class, avoiding gossips and mischief. His lips twisted to the side as he sat thinking, minding his own business. For lunch, he ate plantain chips and drank Fanta. Then he stared through the window and watched other students playing. A thought about Cobra and his friend flashed through his mind. Since their dismissal, he had not seen or heard about them.

When Mona returned home, Pako came to visit him. He drew close to Mona and crossed his legs.

"I have not revised my notes yet. Mum may surprise me by asking me questions on topics I have not mastered well," Mona said.

"Does she do that very often?" Pako asked.

"Yeah."

"When she finds out that you have not revised your notes, what does she do to you?"

"She gets bitter with me."

"Does your dad check your books, too?" Pako asked.

"No, he only advises me to study hard. He is concerned about my position during exams. Mum does most of the work because she is a teacher. But they both always want me to come first."

"My parents want me to come first, too. I don't know why they think it as so easy. I'm in seventh place now."

"It isn't as easy as they think. Mum says she used to be top of the class, and my dad proudly says he, too, used to be number one. I don't know how true that is. I have never seen their report cards. There's nothing to prove that they were as bright as they claim."

"We can't disprove them; it is not right to do so. It seems all parents boast of having been intelligent in their school days. Even those who came last are telling their children that they came first."

"You think everything from America or France is good. Ha, that is colonial mentality!"

"Colonial mentality!" the boy mimicked, scratching his head. "I will check the meaning of the expression when I get back home."

Ma Tata gave the toothpaste to Mona.

"Check its expiry date, my son."

"Mum, it will expire in one year."

"That's OK. How much?" she asked.

"It is two thousand francs, Mum."

"I will give you eight hundred francs, please. Are you OK with that?"

"Mum, I bought it for that same price. If I give it to you at the very price, I would earn nothing."

"OK, I will give one thousand francs so that you can make a profit."

"Thank you. What else do you need, madam? I have balms, hangars, key holders, beer openers, needles, and so on."

"We'll buy them next time." Ma Tata and her son inched along towards the area where women sold vegetables and other foodstuffs.

"Do you know why I brought you to the market?" Ma Tata asked.

"No, Mum."

"I want you to learn how we bargain and buy things here, I want you to avoid being cheated by traders. I hope you have seen how crafty the salesboys are. If you are not wise, they'll sell things to you at high costs."

"I saw that, Mum, and I am learning."
"That's great!"
The vegetable section of the market smelt of spices, leafy greens, and poorly preserved fruits. Saleswomen stacked sheaves of *njamanjama*, edible tubers, onions, and tomatoes on the tables, waiting for buyers. As Ma Tata walked past various tables, women shouted, "Customer, I have good onions. My prices are cheap." Some tried to pull her hand, and she turned and snarled at them.

Finally, Ma Tata stopped at Ma Kata's table, her long-time business partner. With her bright eyes, Ma Kata was lively and buoyant. She wore a torn skirt and oversized rubber boots. Though she, too, played tricks like other sellers, Ma Tata trusted her a bit more.

"Welcome, Ma Teacher," Ma Kata greeted, her face beaming with joy. The saleswoman on her right eyed Ma Kata, then looked away, sighing and shaking her head. "Ma Teacher, I have sweet onions with fine skin and colour. Look at how fleshy they are! My tomatoes were harvested just this morning. And this is the best *njamanjama* from Banso. It is not bitter like what my neighbour is selling. It will pair well with *khati khati*. I also have good bitter leaf for *ndolé.* "

"I am not happy with you, Ma Kata. You sold me bad tomatoes last week."

"I would not do that to you. You are like a blood sister to me."

"I found ten bad ones in the basket."

"Ma Teacher, don't be angry. I am sorry. I didn't see the bad ones. They must have been hiding at the bottom of the basket."

"Yeah, that is what many of you do. You hide rotten foodstuffs at the bottom of your baskets."

"I don't do that, Ma Teacher. I am a God-fearing person."

"Everyone says just that. Besides that, your prices are too high. You must want to lose a faithful customer."

"No, no, Ma Teacher, I can't choose to lose you. I am not responsible for the price increases. Everything is expensive in this country now! We don't know what is happening. Whether it is the wars or something else, I can't tell. We are just managing our own lives in Jesus' name. They say the prices of fertilisers have tripled…"

"I don't want foodstuffs produced with fertilisers," Ma Tata said.

"Ma Teacher, you know me very well. I don't sell anything produced with fertiliser."

"How do you know what is produced with fertiliser? How do you make out the difference?"

"Ma Teacher, I know the farmers and their farms." Ma Tata took a tomato, rolled it in her hand, and pressed it. It was a round, smooth red tomato.

"This looks good. Turn over the basket." All tomatoes from the top to the bottom of the basket were fine. "Mona, put them in the basket, and then fasten the basket in the sack. I don't want them pressed and getting bad on the way home." Ma Tata turned to look at the other items on the table. Large beans in a pail caught her eyes. She grabbed a fistful of black beans and inspected them. They were well dried and winnowed. Apart from their good flavour, black beans blended well with pounded Irish potatoes. Mona loved them with rice. Ma Tata bought spices, beef, and a 25-kilogram bag of Thai rice. Mona stacked all of what was bought in two sacks, stepped back, and looked at the load with wide eyes.

"Mum, the sacks are heavy."

"I know. We won't trek back home. Look for two bikes." The loads were cumbersome, and Mona merely stood and watched how they were loaded onto the bikes. Ma Kata helped the bikers lift the bags. Mona stood looking at her with awe.

"She is very powerful," he said.

"She carries heavy loads every day. Everyone can become perfect at what they do constantly."

Chapter Twelve

Mona Falls Sick

Pako gripped Mona's left arm and they trudged down the slope. Time and again, he halted to let him rest. Mona could barely breathe, and his legs trembled as he walked.

"I think I might vomit," Mona said, snivelling and coughing. Pako guided him towards the gutter, grasping his arm. Mona lifted his head, gasped, and coughed.

"Let's go; I don't feel queasy anymore."

"We ought to take a taxi; you look so feeble." Pako set Mona down on a chair in the sitting room when they got home and got him a glass of water. Mona drank the water and asked for more. After touching his forehead, Pako yelped, "You are too hot! We have to see a doctor at once."

Pa Tata heard voices in the sitting room and came to find out who was talking. When Mona saw him coming, he burst into tears, his face contorting in pain.

"What's happening?" Pa Tata inquired.

"He felt sick at school, so I brought him home," Pako said. Pa Tata came closer and placed a hand on Mona's forehead.

"Be strong of heart, my boy. Stop crying like a baby. Did you eat breakfast?"

"No." Pa Tata went into his room and came out with a bottle of water. In a loud invocation, he sprinkled the water on Mona's forehead.

"Would you like to eat something now?"

"No, I have no appetite."

"You have signs and symptoms of malaria." Pa Tata scurried to the backyard and harvested fresh lemongrass leaves. He washed them in the kitchen, then put them in a bowl, adding slices of ginger and cloves of garlic. Then he put the herbs in a pot with some water and boiled them. He poured three litres of the medicine in a basin and told Mona to inhale the vapour coming out. He poured some in a cup as well and said, "Drink it hot!"

Mona touched the cup and it burnt his hand. "It is too hot," he said, pouting.

Pa Tata fanned the medicine to help it cool quickly. He transferred the liquid into a larger cup and stirred it with a ladle. "It is OK now. Drink it."

Mona tasted a sip of the concoction, and his face twisted in disgust. "It's sour and acidic."

"Drink it. It will heal you."

Mona closed and opened his eyes thrice, looked at the medicine again, and grimaced. At last, he lifted the cup to his mouth and emptied it in two gulps.

"Congrats!" Pa Tata said. Mona's face twisted again as if he had eaten faecal matter. "When the lab tests confirm malaria, you will continue taking this concoction. Herbal medicine kills the malaria germ faster than orthodox medicine. When we come back from the clinic, you will also take *artemisia*. It kills malaria in a matter of seconds."

At the clinic, they met a young trainee nurse at the reception. Dressed in white scrubs and a nursing cap, she looked at them with curious eyes. Mona had stopped shivering but was still unbalanced. The trainee entered his name, address, and age on the consultation card. Then she took his weight and his temperature. Mona saw an unused syringe lying at her table and murmured something negative, thinking perhaps it might be used to inject him.

Distracted by messages on her phone, the nurse delayed them seeing a doctor. She kept scrolling through her phone, sending messages, and making calls. Pa Tata grew impatient with her but kept calm. When at last, she asked Mona to see the doctor, Pa Tata eyed her with disdain but didn't utter a word.

The doctor, dressed in a waist-length jacket, placed his stethoscope on Mona's chest, shifted it to his belly and right down to his groin. After examining his eyes and his heartbeat, he took blood specimens for testing at the lab. Mona's eyes were red, his urine pale yellow.

"We will examine him for malaria and typhoid fever," the doctor told Pa Tata.

"I suspect malaria, Doctor. He doesn't use the mosquito net well. I am sure mosquitoes have infected him with the malaria germ."

"The test results will give us a clue. The results will only be available tomorrow morning because our senior lab technician is on holiday. First thing in the morning, I can assure you, he will get his results. Meantime, I will put him on trial medication. I expect him here at exactly eight o'clock. Eat well before you take the medicine, and drink a lot of water."

"Thank you, Doctor," Pa Tata said.

When they got back home, they met Ma Tata returning from work. Seeing her son in pain, Ma Tata furrowed her forehead, and tiny wrinkles formed above her eyes. Pako hugged her and then explained how Mona had got sick in school.

Ma Tata took a deep breath and looked down.

"He looks very pale," she said, looking at Mona. "Thank you for taking good care of your friend." She patted Pako's back. "Did he obtain permission from school?"

"Yes, he did, Mum," Pako said, stretching his neck, itching to go home. Darkness was coming. The sun glowed red, sinking below the horizon. Ma Tata reached for the kitchen, pulled open the fridge, and peered inside. She opened the lower chamber and took out two moderately ripe papayas. Pako stood at the door, waiting for her expectantly. "Take these." She gave him the papayas. "I am just back from work; we'll eat dinner next time."

"Thank you." Pako gave a broad grin and went off. Ma Tata fixed her eyes on Mona, held his hand firmly and squeezed it in hers. Mona gazed at her lovingly. Embracing him and touching his forehead, she realised that his body was a bit warm.

"How are you feeling now?"
"A bit better."
"Tell me what happened to you in school."
"Before leaving the house in the morning, I had a salty taste in my mouth, but I thought it was normal. I saved my breakfast for long break. At school, I lost my appetite. I got a bitter taste in my mouth, then felt unusually warm. It was then I knew something was wrong with me. I called Pako and offered him my lunch."
"Did you vomit in school?"

"Yes, twice in the school toilet." Ma Tata cuddled his arm in consolation. "It will be OK." She made for Mona's bedroom to check his mosquito net. It was a white rectangular piece of fabric, stretched and fastened to the corners of the bed. Ma Tata saw two holes near the top of the bed, where Mona's head would be as he slept. "Oh, I now see where your problem comes!" She unfastened the net and took it to the sitting room. "You have been sleeping with mosquitoes in your net. Look at these holes."

"I saw them last week."

"Since last week, and you couldn't fix them?" She dashed to the living room to get a needle and thread. Mona watched her neatly patch the holes with little pieces of cloth. "You have been infected by mosquito bites," she said, shaking her head.

That evening, dinner was potato chips with fried eggs. Ma Tata peeled and sliced potatoes, then salted and fried them with eggs. She scarcely cooked a heavy meal after work, except when expecting some guests. "Eat well before taking your drugs," she advised. She got *Supermont* water and kept it beside Mona.

Pa Tata joined them later. As they sat enjoying family time, the Equinox TV news began showing students in handcuffs, dragged along the corridors of a police post. The family stayed mute, watching the images with dismay and listening to the TV reporter. It was a group of students from Lycée de Ngambe who were caught smoking cannabis in an abandoned building near their school. "They will be jailed," Ma Tata suggested.

"Sure," Pa Tata confirmed. Mona kept looking away, feeling ashamed as though he was one of the culprits.

"That's what we are fighting against," Ma Tata said.

The next day, Mona went to the clinic alone for his diagnosis. "You have malaria," the doctor said, looking straight in his eyes. Mona sat quietly in front of him. The doctor gave him tablets and liquid medicine, emphasising the need to take the right dosage. "Eat well before taking your medicine, and drink a lot of water." Mona nodded, put the medicines in his bag, and turned to leave. "Please, don't forget to come back here on Monday."

Feeling slightly queasy, Mona tottered along. On his way home, wherever he felt tired, he rested under a shady tree or sat on a concrete slab. His weight had reduced by two kilos or more.

He came to a busy crossroads and saw a woman selling bananas. Mona gestured to her to come. He noticed that each banana hand in the basket had the same number of fingers. "How much are you selling one hand for?" Mona asked.

"Five hundred francs," the woman said, holding up a hand.

"Hmmm, it is too expensive," Mona said.

"Everything is expensive, my son." She gazed intently at Mona and asked, "Your eyes are red, and you look frail. Are you sick?"

"Yes, Mum. I am from the clinic."

"Oh, I see. Are you a student?"

"Yes, I am, Mum."

"*Ashiaa*! You will get well. How much do you have for the banana?"

"I have two hundred francs."

"I would have given it to you for free, but I have money problems. My landlady is threatening to throw me out of her house for unpaid rent. Give me what you have, my boy. You are a student. Besides, you are ill."

Mona gave her two hundred francs.

"Thank you very much, Mum."

"Don't mention it."

Mona recovered from the malaria disease and was back to school. He made up for lost time by learning from his mates.

Chapter Thirteen

Ma Tata Becomes a Gardener

Owning a garden was one of Ma Tata's greatest dreams. She planned to fulfil the dream when she retired.

Ma Tata had lived with her maternal auntie, who taught her how to garden. She imagined tending her own backyard garden like her auntie, where she could cultivate her own watermelon, tomato, celery, and many other fruits and vegetables.

She envisaged fresh onion leaves swaying on her farm every morning. She dreamt of harvesting ripe tomatoes and eggplants to spice her sauce.

With the rising cost of living and the increase in food prices, waiting for retirement before setting up the horticulture farm seemed foolish. On her last visit to the market, she had spent a fortune on foodstuffs alone. When she got back home, she barely had any of her salary left.

"Could the family income guarantee a good life?" Sitting at her table in the staffroom, the vegetable garden again flashed through her brain, giving her hope.

"On Saturday, we will go back to the market," she told her son. Surprised, Mona raised his head and asked, "Why are we going to the market again so soon, Mum? We still have enough food to last us a week or more."

"We need to set up a vegetable garden." Mona rubbed his hand behind his back.

"I like gardens," he said, holding his mother's hand. "Some of my mates' parents own gardens."

"Times are hard, my son. We can't continue buying everything from the market. We'll only buy what we can't cultivate. I would like to go into my backyard and harvest the bitter leaves I need to prepare my corn *fufu*."

At the market, Ma Tata and her son met Ma Kata, who sprawled on a plastic chair, eating avocado and roast cassava. On seeing her customer, Ma Kata gave a gapped-tooth smile. She wiped her mouth with the edge of her wrapper, washed her hands in a bow, and rose. "Welcome, Ma Teacher," she greeted. "You have returned to the market sooner than I expected. One would think you threw a party with the food you bought last week."

"Ha-ha, I threw no party. What I bought from you is still there. Our school is setting up a garden, and I am in charge of the project."

"Wow, that's great! Won't you cultivate your own garden?" she teased.

"Ma Kata, would you be happy if I had a garden?"

"Why wouldn't I be?"

"If I had a garden, would I still buy vegetables from you?"

"I suppose not, Ma Teacher. But what do you want from me now?"

"For a start, I need seeds for okra, onion, tomato, and *njamanjama*. I also need garlic cloves and fresh scraps of lettuce, cabbage, carrots, and potatoes."

"You must be an expert in garden cultivation."

"I learnt the art from my auntie. She was a well-known gardener who also tended flowers and sold them to businessmen and middle-class people."

Ma Tata bargained and got the seeds at good prices. The scraps were fresh, and she was certain they would produce good vegetables. Ma Tata laid the scraps in a bucket and spread them out to avoid damage, then placed the seedlings in a perforated bag. Mona carried the scraps on his head, walking beside his mother as they returned home.

"Mum, I didn't understand you when you said the garden was for your school."

"Last week, I told you that some traders are crafty. They are interested in profits and nothing else. I think you understand what I am saying."

"I do, Mum."

"If I had told Ma Kata that I intended to grow my own garden, would she have been glad?"

"I don't think so, Mum."

"Good. She would have felt bitter, and sold us spoilt seeds and scraps. She would have frustrated us so that we failed and remained her customers."

"Now I understand you quite well, Mum."

"Do you consider me a liar for telling her the garden was meant for the school?"

"No, no no! You are not a liar!"

"My son, you must be wise, else you get tricked by conmen."

When Ma Tata got ready to launch her garden, fear seized her heart: fear of wandering animals eating her vegetables. Some of her neighbours owned grass-eating animals, too, who sometimes escaped and destroyed crops on people's farms. To secure her vegetables, she decided to build a fence round the garden. She got pickets, dug holes, and positioned them in the ground. Then she fastened cane ropes to the pickets to ensure no animal trespassed the garden. At one corner of the garden, she created a small bamboo door and locked it with a padlock.

Ma Tata made elevated ridges, which looked like mounds, and placed a mixture of organic fertilisers on each ridge: cattle manure, poultry droppings, and decomposed plants. She detested chemical fertilisers, arguing that they were expensive and destructive to the soil. Ma Tata didn't bother acquiring a fountain, though a fountain might be necessary if the garden needed a lot of water in the future. She cultivated some vegetables, working hard to ensure they blossomed well and were not attacked by pests. Evening morning, she went to the garden with Mona, watered the stalks and roots of plants, spread manure on ridges, weeded, and pruned withered leaves. Every evening, she prayed for good yield.

Chapter Fourteen

Mona Passes the GCE -Level

As years slipped away, the food crisis persisted in Kibanki. At the various markets, prices kept increasing, at times due to poor economic policies, or because of conspiracies from the traders themselves. Traders doubled prices for personal gain. Most of them amassed a lot of wealth by driving sharp bargains. The markets were filled with goods, and every saleable item bore a highprice tag. Ma Tata didn't bother spending money on fruitsor vegetables. Her garden had flourished, so she spent herearnings on other needs.

Mona was in his final year at school. By the end of June, he would sit the GCE O-Level. Time flew like a hungry hawk. Mona was still boyish and agile — his chin was bare of any beard — though his voice had deepened with age. He had also been blessed with marvellous athletic abilities.

The GCE writing session was close at hand. Mona and Pako joined three other classmates and formed a study group, which they named "The Big Six." The group was reserved for above-average students who were committed, disciplined, and hardworking. Ma Tata warned them to guard against lazy students. To respect gender balance, the group comprised three girls and three boys. They met thrice a week in Mona's house, practised drawing, typed on the computer, solved maths problems, conjugated verbs in English and French, and read passages loud. Before every meeting, the members agreed on what would be studied during the next session. They also agreed on who would coordinate each session. Science subjects got particular attention, and those good at them were encouraged to help the weak ones with drills and exercises.

Ma Tata advised Mona to prepare well for his exam.

"Yesterday your study mates spent the whole time telling stories. I hope they are not coming here for a story contest."

"We studied before telling stories. We only tell stories when we have finished our work."

"Why do you tell stories, by the way? Are you training to become writers?"

"We say riddles and recount tales to entertain ourselves and drive off stress."

It was the rainy season, and Mona intensified his studies at home.

"During exams, you will sit and think alone, and interpret and answer questions alone. And if you fail, you fail alone. If you pass, you pass alone. An exam is like death; you don't die with anyone." Mona liked studying at dawn when the house was quiet, when he heard no shrills of insects, no squeaks of rodents, no chirps of birds, no whizzes of nocturnal winds. He adored the chilly, fragrant night air, which swirled in the living room, though mosquitoes sometimes stood in his way.

When Mona woke, the crisp morning air refreshed him. He sat in an aging ebony chair in the living room, taking gentle breaths. To study for several hours without feeling weary, Mona sat up straight, kept his feet flat on the floor, relaxed his shoulders, and kept his elbows close to his body. His energy waned when he sat in a relaxed posture. A white rechargeable lamp stood at one corner of the table, lighting his books so he could read. It was the only source of light during blackouts. Every day, without warning, blackouts affected various households.

Mona's study methods differed as each was adopted for a particular purpose. Slowly but surely, he studied each topic line by line, pointing out key facts, and then digesting them accordingly. Though this method proved to be time-consuming and strenuous, Mona knew it was more effective in retaining information. Some of his teachers were revising for exams, and he knew there was still room to catch up.

All was tranquil at home. Mona perched in a rocking chair, relaxing. His cell phone chimed. When he answered, the caller spoke hastily and then hung up. Mona perked up his ears like a rabbit. The call came from a noisy area, and the caller stuttered as he spoke. However, Mona heard the last words spoken, "You have passed the GCE!"

Mona thought the young voice was one of his classmates. His eyes sparkled, and relief filled him. "If this is true, how many subjects have I passed?"

He dialled the number to no avail; the phone was switched off for the moment. He felt like shouting, leaping, but a sudden fear subdued his emotions. Many a candidate had rejoiced in the past and ended up crying. As he stood confused, his mind shrouded in doubt, Pa Tata approached, a big smile brightening his face. Mona had never seen him so happy.

"Congrats, my son!" Mona leapt and grasped him in a tight embrace. They stood holding each other for a few seconds.

"I am very happy, my son. You make me proud." Tears of joy ran down Mona's cheeks, wetting his T-shirt. After a few moments, Pako trotted in, panting. "We have made it," he said, embracing Pa Tata. Mona lifted up Pako despite being lighter weight. They smiled from ear to ear.

"You eat kola nuts, don't you?" Pa Tata asked.

"We don't," they chorused.

"I have pineapple juice. Would you like some?" The boys nodded. Pa Tata darted to his living room and came out with the juice. "You deserve red feathers," he said, giving them the juice. With gleeful faces, they sat drinking and chatting.

"I called you a few minutes ago," Pako said.

"Ah, I couldn't make out your voice. You were in a noisy place."

"Sure. I used my mum's phone."

When Ma Tata returned from work, Mona jumped for joy, his heart racing. He held her Mum and hugged her. Pako came and joined the hug and they squeezed her. "Congrats, my sons!" After letting go of her, they whistled and hopped about like ravens. "The GCE Board has released the results early this year," Ma Tata said.

Mona and Pako called "The Big Six" while Ma Tata went to the bedroom and changed her dress. She sat on her bed and reflected for a brief moment. "What will I prepare for supper?"

She went to the kitchen. The small portion of pork in the oven could not serve five visitors. She got the chicken in the freezer, sliced and boiled it in the aluminium pot. *Garri* with tomato sauce would be pretty good for supper, she thought. She engrossed herself in the cooking, clanking pots and cutlery as she stirred her sauce in a hurry.

Pa Tata came inside, pulling along a cumber-some crate, filled with soda and beer bottles. Mona helped his father by taking the crate and placing it beside the dining table. As they stood, exchanging joyful laughs, Pako's father Mr Pefok emerged from the front yard. Casually dressed in a pink T-shirt over a pair of blue jeans, he walked up the steps, smiling pleasantly. Ma Tata recognised his voice and came out to greet him. She exchanged warm pleasantries with him and returned to the kitchen.

"Our children have done it!" Mr Pefok said.

"They are the winners of tomorrow. Can you believe that they all passed?" Pa Tata said.

"Their hard work has paid off." Pa Tata got a bottle of beer, uncorked it, and gave to Mr Pefok. They sat drinking and laughing. Pako returned home to change his clothes. Ma Tata continued cooking, and Mona helped her by setting the table.

A couple of minutes later, Pa Mo walked in, dressed in a jumper, wearing a *kufi* hat, a *ndop* jacket, and rubber sandals. Upon seeing him, Mr Pefok sighed.

"What is this man coming here for?" he asked Pa Tata.

"He is a regular visitor to this home."

"No, please! You don't do that! You are hiding a serpent with fangs under your bed."

"Who is a serpent?" Pa Mo cut in, moving closer to Mr Pefok.

"You are one, sir. A thief! I won't say this behind your back. I must say it to your face, and I won't mince any of my words."

"Mind your words, swine! Can you prove what you are saying, my friend?"

"I can prove it. You are a disgusting person."

"Look at you! You call yourself a teacher. Are you an effective teacher? If you are, why are your products prowling about, breaking into houses, scamming and gambling?"

"I prefer teaching to scaling hedges and stealing goats and pigs. People like you have shown them shortcuts to earn money, what do you expect?"
Pa Mo raised his walking stick and made to hit Mr Pefok. "Oh, no fighting!" Pa Tata shouted, standing between the two.

"Pa Tata, if you allow this man to be part of this feast, I will leave. What will this old rogue tell our kids? Let him go and preside over feasts for gangsters!"

"Please, be calm. You are addressing him harshly. Mark you, he is old enough to be your father."

"Pa Tata, I have no problem with his age. I am a child of Kibanki, and we are known for respecting elders. But we were never told to respect elderly thieves."

"Pa Tata, you have offered me a seat, but I won't sit because of this gadfly. Let me go back to my house. If I insist on staying here, I will likely exchange fists with this naughty swine passing for a teacher. I don't know what he teaches. I will never send any of my children to a school where this fellow teaches. When you invite underage female students to pleasure centres, what do you teach them there?"

"Pa Mo, have a seat. You have come to visit me, not Mr Pefok."

He gnashed his teeth, spat, and turned to go.

"Pa Mo, I have not sent you away from my home."

"You can't do so because you are a gentleman. I am sorry, I must leave because of this skunk who calls himself an educator. Let this man educate his own mind first before aspiring to educate anybody."

"Bravo! I am glad the famous thief is leaving. Our goats might be safe for today," Mr Pefok said, chuckling and sipping his beer.

"I don't want to curse you because you are already under a curse."

"A serpent's curse does not work anywhere. I insult you without fear because I know you can't curse me. Don't waste precious time thinking you can curse anyone here."

"When I look at you, I pity the woman sitting somewhere thinking she has a son." Pa Tata gave Pa Mo a bottle of 33 Export, whispering to him, "Don't be annoyed, Mr Pefok is certainly drunk. He has swilled six bottles of Kadji Beer." Pa Mo turned and looked at Pefok with wicked eyes. He grabbed his walking stick, grumbling as he walked off.

At exactly seven o'clock, "The Big Six" came to visit Mona. The girls sat at the centre of the living room, all dressed in sleeveless velvet party blouses. Each blouse matched perfectly with white socks and low-heeled shoes. Violet headbands hung graciously on each of their heads, sparkling in the lamplight. The hairstyles were similar, so too, were their make-up, their perfume, and jewellery. Looking at them, Ma Tata nodded. She found no fault with their attire. The boys dressed modestly: black jeans, Adidas T-shirts, and tennis shoes. None of them wore a cap, and none wore cologne.

Pa Tata and Mr Pefok sat at the dining table, drinking beer and cracking jokes.

Soft music turned on. Ma Tata made a short speech, congratulating the students on their success amid applauses and loud laughter. Pa Tata said a short prayer and told the students to keep working hard. He gave examples of people who rose from poverty to glory through devotion and effort. Mr Pefok was slightly stupefied from the alcohol. He perched on his seat unashamed. No one called out his excesses. Enraged and embarrassed, Pako looked away, shaking his head.

Food was served in transparent glass dishes. Everyone dug in.

After supper, it was time for dancing. The girls jumped onto the floor as their favourite beats sounded from the loudspeakers. Ma Tata observed, her gaze steady on their body movements. Without overdoing the dance, they bent, rose, sank, jumped, glided and twisted, while smiling and laughing. Excited, Ma Tata rose, darted forward and showered them with banknotes. The boys joined the dance but not as smoothly as the girls. Ma Tata joined in, jumping, raising her hands and shaking her waist like a weaverbird. The audience laughed and applauded, and she intensified her body movements to greater effect. Smiles spread across everyone's face. At midnight, the feast came to a halt, and everyone retired.

Chapter Fifteen

Glorious News for the Family

As a teacher, Ma Tata knew a great deal about the employment problem in her country. Hundreds of thousands of qualified people chased jobs. Jobseekers flocked into offices with angry and saddened faces, carrying files with copies of their school certificates. With sad and hopeless looks, they queued up for employment services, submitting handwritten applications, many of which were never read. When the personnel managers got bored with piles of applications stacked before them, they simply ordered their secretaries to dump them in the dustbins. Jobs were scarce, and only a few persons got employed, most often through connections, bribery, or corruption.

"Mona will train for two years, then come back and work with us," Ma Tata said. Pa Tata nodded.

"It's a bright decision," he said. "He'll gain much knowledge in the school of veterinary medicine. After his training, he will know about animal feed, diseases, and so on."

"The best thing in these times is to be self-employed," Ma Tata said.

"I have talked to Mr Pefok about professional training and he is okay with it. As soon as Pako obtains his A-Level, he too, will go to the school of veterinary medicine."

"That's a good idea! If you aren't creative today, you'll perish." With the loan obtained from a credit union, Pa Tata added more pigs to his pigsty. He cleared the land to enlarge the pen. Eighteen pigs of different breeds inhabited the sty. Some of them bore dotted marks on their bodies, and others had flat snouts. The sty was noisy as pigs stamped their hooves and grunted. Pa Tata also bought pigeons, hens, and roosters. Ma Tata used the fowl droppings and pig dung as manure for her garden. She too had enlarged her garden by planting more flowers and fruit trees. The garden flourished with fresh fruits and leafy vegetables.

On her day off, Ma Tata was in the garden, tugging weeds from the ridges. Her phone rang and she answered. "Hello?"

"Congratulations on your appointment!"

"What appointment, sir?" she asked, raising her eyebrows.

"Watch the six p.m. news on the National TV. You have been appointed as the principal of GHS Kibanki." Ma Tata placed a hand on her chest, unable to speak. She darted to the house.

"Are you OK?" Pa Tata asked.

"My principal called and told me I have been appointed as the principal of GHS Kibanki.

I am not so certain. We need confirmation."

"You think your principal goes about kidding like a lad?"

"My doubt is justified, my husband. You don't move straight from a teaching position to principal. There is a formal procedure to follow. First, you are promoted to master of discipline. From there, you move up to a senior master of discipline. Then vice principal, and finally, you may become a principal."

"Are you saying nobody has gone from a teacher to a principal?"

"I know a few cases, and most of them have been the children of grandees like attorneys, barons, deputies, senators, governors and ministers."

"Don't forget that you have been doing great things as a trade unionist. You certainly have been rewarded for that role."

"I thought of that as well." It was dusk and the news was making the rounds in Kibanki. Ma Tata's phone chirped every minute.

"Congratulations, Ma Teacher!" Ma Kata shouted from the market.

Mr Pefok called, praising the promotion. At nightfall, Ma Tata's phone battery ran down because she received many calls. Radio Bright broadcast the news, giving a detailed biography of Ma Tata. The appointment was captioned on major news channels the next day. Bloggers and social media influencers dug out Ma Tata's biography and published it.

The front page of the *Post* newspaper wrote, "Ma Tata Becomes the New Principal of GHS Kibanki." The *Herald* newspaper passed on the news more subtly: "A Famous Trade Unionist Takes over GHS Kibanki."

Mona was at school, staying in the dormitory. Informed about the promotion, he called his mother and chanted praise, promising to come and participate in the installation ceremony. At night, his friends came and lifted Ma Tata on their shoulders, singing songs of conquest. "Welcome to our school. You are the winner!" they chorused.

As Ma Tata and her husband sat in the living room talking, a stumpy man knocked on the door and entered. It was their landlord's elder brother, dressed in ragged clothes. His sharp eyes made his face unfriendly.

"Welcome," Pa Tata greeted. The man refused to sit.

"I am your landlord's elder brother," he said proudly.

"We know you," Ma Tata said.

"I sponsored my younger brother. I spent a huge sum of money to have him recruited into the army; I made him what he is today. Now I am wretched, and he is enjoying life with his wife and children."

"Sir, what is our concern about all that?" Pa Tata asked.

"His house is my house. He is my blood brother, take note."

"I think you should see your brother and talk with him," Ma Tata said.

"Why should I see him? I have the right to evict you from this house without asking his opinion."

"Sir, be calm. We signed no contract with you, and we don't owe rent here," Pa Tata said.

"You have turned my brother's land into a farm. Do you pay extra rent for rearing dirty animals and setting up gardens here?"

"We can't bear this any longer!" Ma Tata said, standing up. "I will call the police," she threatened. The man heard the word "police" and got scared. He ran off.

"I told you that your appointment will bring jealousy from all angles," Pa Tata said.

"I will ask the landlord to warn his brother. If he sets foot here again, he will face the law," Ma Tata said, clenching her teeth.

Chapter Sixteen

The Thief Visits

Though her new job was demanding, Ma Tata pledged to be devoted and hardworking. Back from school one afternoon, she slouched on a lounge chair beside the threshold, relaxing. A soft twinkle came to her eyes as the sunrays warmed her tense muscles. Her recent appointment had brought joy to her heart. As she sat radiating with happy memories, her landlord emerged from the front yard, a deep frown on his face. "Good afternoon, Ma Tata," he greeted.

"Hello, sir."

"Congratulations on your appointment."

"Thank you." Ma Tata rose and shook hands with him.

"You deserve the job, and I know you will address the school's issues."

"Thank you, sir." Ma Tata knew what was bothering the landlord as he kept fixing his eyes at her. She stood quiet, waiting for him to express his worry.

"Ma Tata, I was quite upset when you told me that my brother came here and threatened to evict you from this house."

"He also said a lot of horrible things about you."

"I know he mocked and shamed my name. But this is not his land. He has no right to this house. A one-sided story is always a twisted story, that's why I came to give you my own side."

"He told us he sponsored you and you have never reciprocated his goodwill."

"He did sponsor me, and so what? Is he the first person to sponsor a family member? I am sponsoring his son at GHS Kibanki. Does that not balance the deal? When I offer him money, he takes it to the bars and makes merry with friends and loose girls."

"When I threatened to call the police, he fled."

"You did the right thing. He's scared of policemen. He fought with a friend one day, and the police locked him up and tortured him."

"I see," Ma Tata said, laughing. "I hope he won't come here again."

"I can assure you, he won't."

The next day, Ma Tata was at school. Pa Tata had gone in search of animal feed. When Pa Tata came back from the feed mill, a wave of fear crept down his spine. An invisible voice told him that something had gone wrong in the pigsty. Gripped with fear, he flung the feed by the door and sprinted to the sty. There were fresh footmarks around the pig fence. Bewildered, he counted the pigs. Five pigs were missing. A steadier recount still showed a shortage. Perplexed, Pa Tata shook his head and clenched his fists. "Someone has stolen from me," he shouted.

He rushed to Pa Mo's house as he considered him the prime suspect in the theft. "Where's Pa Mo?" he asked.

"He travelled," a little girl said. She was Pa Mo's lastborn. With a cheerful face and low-cut hair, she looked bold and smart.

"When did he travel?"

"Just when I came back from school."

"Was he alone?"

"Yes."

"Did you see him with any pigs?"

"No." Pa Tata spat and rubbed his hand on his chin. He walked away slowly, shaking his head and grumbling to himself.

Pa Tata drummed his fingers on the table as he saw Ma Tata coming back from school. He swallowed hard before he delivered the bad news.

"Five pigs are gone," Pa Tata told her, wincing. Tears filled her eyes, and her chin trembled. She leaned against the pig fence, staring at the remaining pigs. The big sow had been stolen alongside four other pigs.

"My goodness! Who did this to us? Have you checked on Pa Mo?"

"Yeah. They said he has travelled somewhere."

"Aha! You have been nursing a serpent calling it a friend." The safe pigs snorted with hunger and thirst. Ma Tata called the police and reported the incident. She got a bottle of water and gulped it down. Pa Tata stood at the edge of the sty, strewing feed to the remaining pigs. A while later, two police constables, dressed in blue khaki trousers and jackets arrived in a van. With stern faces, they observed the thieves' trails and wrote the incident down. "I suspect Pa Mo," Pa Tata told them.

"Who is Pa Mo?" the taller constable asked.

"He is my neighbour," Pa Tata explained.

"Why do you think he is the one who stole your pigs?"

"He is a famous thief. When anything goes missing here, he is the first suspect."

"Show us his house." When the constables got to Pa Mo's house, they saw nobody. They went back in the evening, and he was still not there.

The next day, some students from GHS Kibanki said they saw Pa Mo on the day of the theft, sweating as he pulled pigs across Kibanki's border. Cobra and Sango were assisting him. The trio wore flat caps, which covered part of their faces. They had wrapped mufflers round their necks and walked cautiously. For three days, Pa Mo was seen nowhere in Kibanki.

"We need a guard," Ma Tata said.

"You are right. We need one urgently."

"You didn't listen to me at the beginning. I told you not to trust Pa Mo. When we brought in more animals, I asked you to recruit a guard."

"Mr Pefok assured me yesterday that he will bring me a guard in less than twenty-four hours. He knows of someone who is ready to take the job."

"That is good."

Pa Tata hired a barrel-chested guard to look after the animals, the garden, and the chickens. Bastara was a former athletic champion and holder of a black belt in Tai Chi, Kung Fu. With his hostile looks, he made the Tatas' residence a no-go area. His weapons were a bow and arrow, a catapult, a butcher's knife, a blunt machete, and a spear. During daytime, he went round the sty, inspecting and guarding the pigs. Every night, he walked the border of the compound, flashing his torchlight around to scare away thieves.

A week later, Pa Mo was seen in Kato by a Kibanki local, still in the company of Cobra and Sango. They were seen lounging on a seaside terrace, having a rowdy time with strangers, swilling and offering beer to whoever needed it. Cobra and Sango wore bowties, sparkling shirts, black trousers, and white shoes. Pa Mo wore a black cassock, which descended to his toes and covered his sandals. Cobra and Sango silently looked around and concentrated on their drinks. Four girls with generous bottoms sandwiched them, three of them sitting close to Pa Mo, whispering to him, smiling, and asking from him countless favours.

"You promised to buy me a Christmas gown," one of the girls said. She cuddled Pa Mo, and he smiled broadly.

"I will give you the money later. I don't want others to see me giving you money," he whispered to the girl.

Another girl with a beautiful face and thick lips tapped Pa Mo on the head and said, "I want to drink Campari." On Pa Mo's order, a barmaid brought a sparkling bottle of Campari and set it on the table. The girl laughed, served herself, and took a sip. Another girl asked for roasted meat, and it was brought and served in a silver dish. Happiness bloomed inside Pa Mo's heart as the girls cheered his name.

When Pa Tata heard the news of the merrymaking in Kato, he buried his face in his hands and took a deep breath. A freezing sense of shame crossed his mind.

As Ma Tata stooped in her garden, weeding out scrap grass from the ridges, Mr Pefok emerged from near the house. "They have been arrested!" he shouted, panting. Ma Tata's eyes grew wide as she leapt to her feet. "You mean Pa Mo and his gang?"

"Yes! The Kibanki police picked them up in Kato last night. They are in custody, and it is rumoured they will be moved to the Kibanki Maximum Prison, pending trial."

"Good news!" she waved her head and grinned.

"My fear is that Pa Mo might buy his way out as usual."

"I'm not sure he will succeed this time. I will personally make sure they pay for their deeds. "

Printed in the United States
by Baker & Taylor Publisher Services